cious

ALBUQUERQUE/BERNALILLO
COUNTY LIBRARIES

AL

RIO GRANDE VALLEY
LIBRARY SYSTEM

Withdrawn/ABCL

RIO GRANDE VALLEY
LIBRARY SYSTEM

Annie and
Cousin Precious

Annie and Cousin Precious

Kay Chorao

DUTTON CHILDREN'S BOOKS   NEW YORK

3 9075 01576 6022

RIO GRANDE VALLEY
LIBRARY SYSTEM

Copyright © 1994 by Kay Sproat Chorao

All rights reserved.

CIP Data is available.

Published in the United States 1994 by
Dutton Children's Books,
a division of Penguin Books USA Inc.
375 Hudson Street, New York, New York 10014

Designed by Riki Levinson

Printed in Hong Kong   First edition
10 9 8 7 6 5 4 3 2 1   ISBN 0-525-45238-9

In memory of the real Annie

ousin Precious howled on the doorstep.
Annie sulked in her bedroom.

Papa was at his wit's end. He knocked on Annie's door.
"Annie, come out," he said.

"No," said Annie.

"Now," said Papa in a louder voice. "Cousin Precious is
sitting all by herself. She wants to play."

"No," said Annie.

Papa threw open Annie's door.

"I am ashamed of you," he said, his eyes like black mar-
bles. "Cousin Precious has come to visit, and you won't play
with her. That is not nice."

"But I don't want her here. She ruins everything."

Cousin Precious tippy-tapped into the room. A big pink bow bobbed on her head. It matched the pink bows on her shoes. Tippy-tap, tippy-tap.

"I want to play in Annie's playhouse, but she won't let me," said Precious. When Papa wasn't looking she stuck out her little pink tongue at Annie.

"I built that playhouse for you to share," said Papa, frowning at Annie.

"But she'll mess up everything and break things."

"You take her there right now," barked Papa.

Slowly Annie got up. Slowly she trudged down the stairs, out the door, and across the lawn.

She led the way to a shed attached to the big old barn at the end of a drive.

"This is the playhouse," announced Annie. "See? It is just a shed. Now we can go back."

Precious stamped her foot and began to howl. "I'll tell on you," she cried.

"All right," said Annie, stretching up and sliding open the bolt.

The door swung open.

"Ooooooooh," said Precious, wide-eyed.

Inside it wasn't like a shed at all. It was like a real little house, with tiny rooms and cozy furniture, books, and even a miniature kitchen with shelves and doll dishes. Papa had worked for months making this magical world.

Precious closed her mouth, which had fallen open in astonishment. She narrowed her eyes and tippy-tapped through the door.

"Where are the dollies?" she demanded.

"Beary is napping in the cradle," said Annie. "He's my favorite."

"Ugh," said Precious. "A bear with a button nose. Don't you have any real dollies?"

"I have Roberta and Alfredo," said Annie, pointing to a high chair.

"You have dumb dolls. I have lots and lots of dollies. And they aren't homemade like yours. They are real plastic dollies from department stores."

"Then just go home and play with your plastic dolls," cried Annie.

"No, and you can't make me," said Precious. She grabbed Roberta and Alfredo. The high chair slammed to the floor. Then she snatched Beary from his cradle.

"We will give all the children a bath now," she ordered, running to the kitchen.

"No!" cried Annie. "My dollies can't get wet. They'll fall apart!" She rushed to rescue her dolls.

"You can't have them. *I* am playing with them," said Precious, dodging Annie and bumping into a bookcase.

Books crashed to the floor.

"My books!" cried Annie.

"Never mind," said Precious, still holding the dolls. "We will just have a little dance, children."

Precious began to dance and spin around the room, with the dolls dragging on the floor.

"Stop!" wailed Annie. "You'll rip them!"

"Dance, children, dance," sang Precious, spinning and tapping, faster and faster.

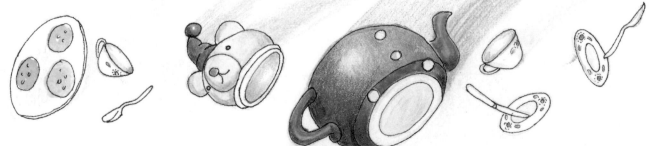

"If you don't stop, I'm going to leave," said Annie.

Precious wasn't listening. She was too busy dancing and spinning.

"I'm *leaving,*" said Annie. But Precious didn't hear her.

Annie ran out the door and bolted it. Then she ran into the barn and peered through a knothole in the wall of the horse's stall. She could see Precious in the shed on the other side of the wall.

"That was a good dance," said Precious. She dumped the dolls in a pile and picked up a book. "Now we will read, children. Once upon a time there was a beeeeee-oo-tiful princess. Her name was *Precious.*"

"Who was turned into a brussels sprout by her cousin," yelled Annie through the knothole.

Precious dropped the book and began to run around the playhouse. "Are we playing hide-and-seek?" she asked.

"We are playing *invisible*," yelled Annie.

"You aren't fooling me. Come out now," said Precious.

"No, there is a Playhouse Monster who turns everyone invisible," said Annie.

"I don't believe you," said Precious. "Where are you?"

Annie scratched the horse in his favorite spot. He stomped his feet, which was his way of asking for more.

Stomp. Stomp. Stomp.

"That is the Playhouse Monster. He has giant stompy feet and big black teeth," yelled Annie through the knothole.

"You're scaring me, Annie," whined Precious.

"Good," said Annie. Then she marched out of the barn, past Papa in his bakery, and up to her room, leaving Precious still running in circles.

It was quiet in Annie's room. No tippy-tapping. No boss-
ing. No howling. Just quiet. For a while she played. Then
she looked out the window. The sun had slipped behind
black clouds. It was a little dark. Precious would be more and
more frightened. She wouldn't be able to open the door.
What if she smashed a window to get out and hurt herself?
Oh, oh.

Annie ran down the stairs. She ran across the lawn and
down the drive to the shed. No broken windows. Precious
must be inside. But the door was unbolted.

Slowly Annie pushed open the door. "Precious?" she
called. No answer.

What if a monster really *did* come? thought Annie. Would
he gobble her up? Oh, oh.

Now Annie was scared. Precious was her youngest cousin, and she had teased her and frightened her and made something awful happen.

On the floor next to Beary and Roberta, Annie found a big pink bow. She picked it up. Looking at the bow made tears come to Annie's eyes.

She ran to Papa's bakery.

"Well, Annie, what do you have to say for yourself?" asked Papa.

"I lost Precious," whispered Annie.

"Oh, dear," said Papa. "That is serious."

"I didn't mean to lose her. I'm sorry." Annie tried to wipe away her tears.

"Well, if we find her again, will you take better care of her?" asked Papa.

"Yes, if she doesn't boss me and ruin my things," said Annie.

"Then let's see if we can find her," said Papa.

He bent down and reached for something behind the pie case. When he stood up, he was holding Precious. "Look who I found, crying in the playhouse."

"You were bad, Annie," announced Precious, stuffing the remains of a raspberry pie in her mouth.

"You were bad, too," said Annie. "I thought something awful had happened to you, and it would have been all my fault."

"I *knew* you liked me a little," said Precious.

"I didn't say *that*," said Annie.

Precious drooped sadly, hugging Alfredo. "Alfredo likes me. He kept me from being too scared. Can he be my special doll till I go home?"

"If you promise to bring some plastic dollies next time, so we can give them real baths," said Annie.

"Next time? Next time?" said Precious, hopping up and down. "Next time means I can come again. Next time means you *do* like me a little." She grabbed Annie's paw.

"If you don't boss and if you don't howl, I will show you the real Playhouse Monster," said Annie.

Then before Precious could say no, Annie pulled her out the door.

They raced to the barn, where they made the horse stomp, stomp, stomp. And Precious showed Annie how to tippy-tap.

Then they all stomped and tapped and tapped and stomped until the rafters shook.